ALPACA POE

WRITTEN BY

Susan Cortz

ILLUSTRATED BY

Jamie Cortz

ISBN: 979-8-9874537-0-4
LCCN: 2023903452

 Published by Humming Oaks Press.
www.hummingoakspress.com

Printed in the U.S.A.

The artwork for this book was created with acrylic paint on watercolor paper and digital media.
The type is set in Calluna.

To Mom and Dad,
whose wise words inspired this book,
and to Jamie, who brought my story to life.

Alpaca Poe was quite a sight,
with crooked, knobby knees
and giant eyes with lashes that
would flutter in the breeze.

He stood no taller than a goat.
His fleece had one white streak.
Combined, he was a charming blend
of quirky and unique.

Though gentle, Poe was strong at heart.
While spunky, he was sweet
and radiated kindness from
his head to two-toed feet.

Poe lived on Windy Willows Farm,
a peaceful friendly place
with shady trees, an old red barn,
and miles of open space.

He played and grazed beside his mom,
who taught him truths she knew
would help him through life's challenges
and guide him as he grew.

Poe loved his Windy Willows home
and never thought there'd be
a day that he would have to leave
his friends and family.

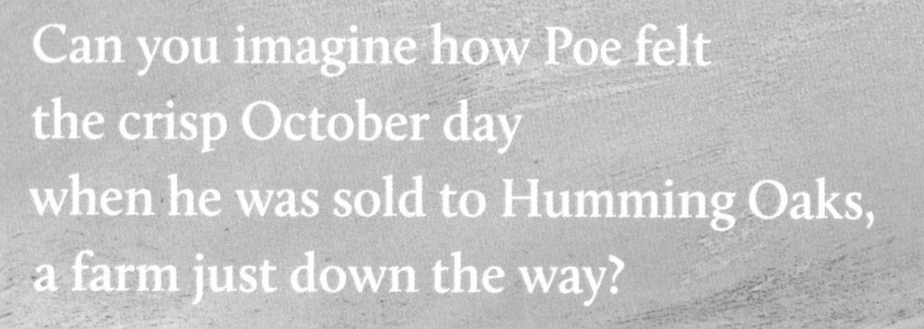

Can you imagine how Poe felt
the crisp October day
when he was sold to Humming Oaks,
a farm just down the way?

Without a warning, he'd been caught,
was haltered, and then stuck
inside a trailer pulled behind
the farmer's big red truck.

His mom called as the engine roared,
"Although we'll live apart,
we'll always be together, Poe,
inside each other's heart."

Through teary eyes, poor helpless Poe
watched Windy Willows fade
as he was whisked to his new home,
heartbroken and afraid.

When Poe arrived at Humming Oaks,
he looked around to see
some strange alpacas trotting up
to see who he might be.

A few feet from the place he stood,
they all just stopped and gawked.
They thought Poe looked so strange and small;
some laughed and some looked shocked.

“What crooked legs!”

“His eyes are HUGE!”

“He’s just a little squirt!”

“He looks like an enormous skunk!”

With each word,
Poe's heart hurt.

Poe thought of what his mom might say;
her words rang wise and true.
“They don’t know, yet, how great you are—
that part is up to you.”

So, bravely, Poe approached the group
and asked them, “May I play?”
They formed a huddle to decide,
then shouted out, “NO WAY!”

NO!

"You've got bug eyes!"
"Your stripe is weird!"
"You're not like one of us!"

Poor Poe was crushed by their cruel words
but left without a fuss.

The others teased and picked on Poe
and left him on his own,
although they knew herd animals
should never be alone.

His mom's voice whispered in his head
as he lay feeling blue,
"Continue to be good and kind
no matter what they do.

It's harder to be kind than mean,
but you are strong and brave.
Your good example may just change
the way that they behave."

So every day, he'd say nice things and smile at everyone.

"Good morning!"

"Howdy!"

"How are you?"

"Gesundheit!"

"Nicely done!"

Poe's herdmates didn't understand
his upbeat attitude.
They thought he must have lost his mind
and kept on being rude.

But rather than feel sad or mope,
Poe found creative ways
to lift his drooping spirits up
and pass the lonely days.

He'd spy cloud creatures in the sky,
watch squirrels steal nuts like thieves,
admire friendly ladybugs,
and chase the blowing leaves.

Each night he'd watch for shooting stars
before he counted sheep,
then dreamed of Windy Willows and
his mom as he would sleep.

And as the days turned into weeks,
he kept up his routine,
preferring his own company
to herdmates that were mean.

Until....

As Poe lay down one night, he saw
coyotes in a pack.
He knew he had to help his herd
before they could attack.

Without a thought about himself,
Poe ran, with all his might,
directly at the pack just like
a phantom in the night.

He made a screechy high pitched-hum
that caused the pack alarm
and woke up all the animals
asleep around the farm.

They saw coyotes run away
through unbelieving eyes.
"Who's that?" one asked.
"It's Poe!" one said.
"So brave for his small size!"

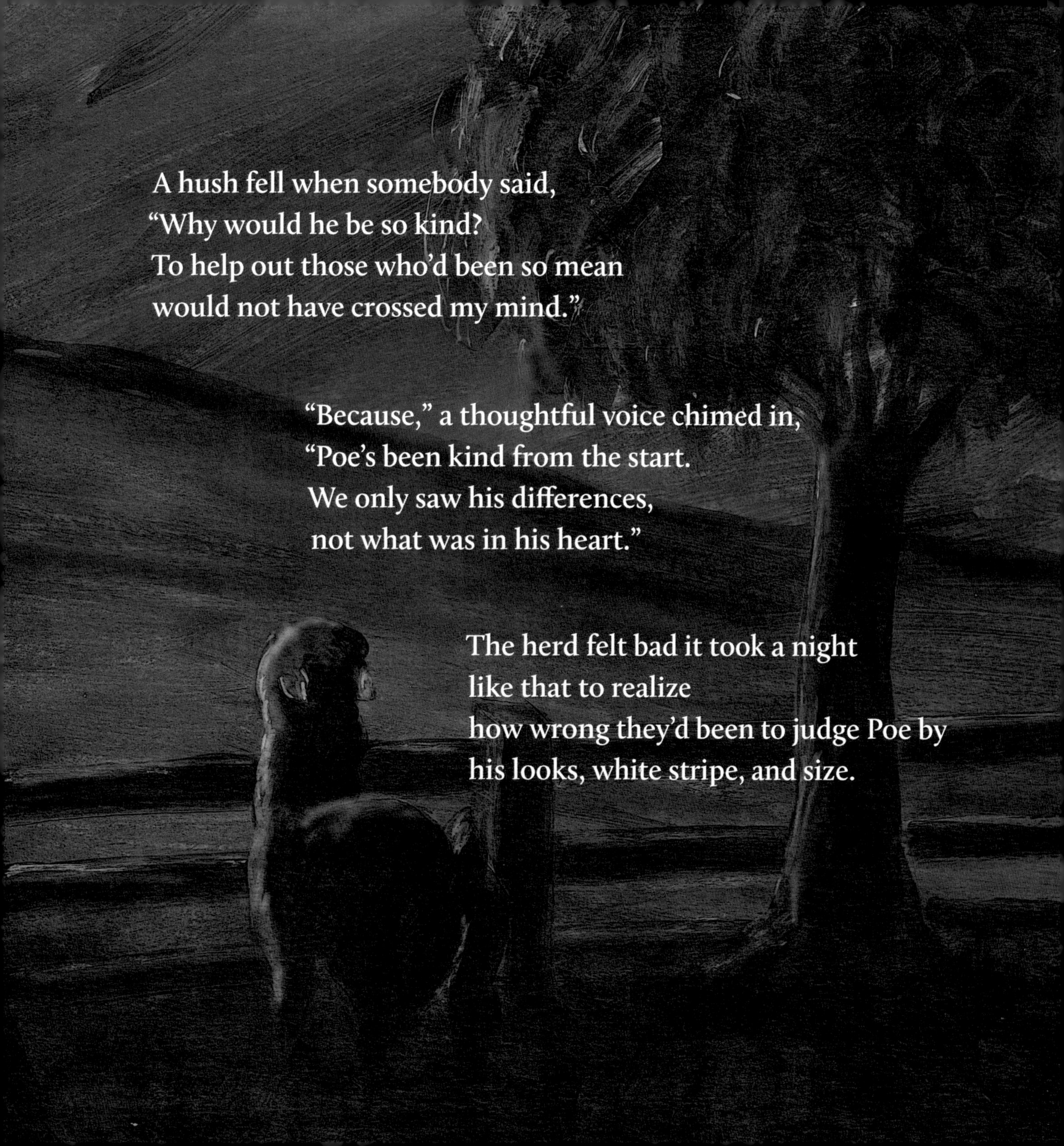

A hush fell when somebody said,
"Why would he be so kind?
To help out those who'd been so mean
would not have crossed my mind."

"Because," a thoughtful voice chimed in,
"Poe's been kind from the start.
We only saw his differences,
not what was in his heart."

The herd felt bad it took a night
like that to realize
how wrong they'd been to judge Poe by
his looks, white stripe, and size.

By never changing who he was,
he'd helped his herd's hearts grow.
They now choose friends for *who* they are,
thanks to Alpaca Poe.

Made in the USA
Las Vegas, NV
26 February 2024